E   Vigna, Judith
VIG
      Boot weather

$13.95

DATE			

BOOT WEATHER

Story and pictures by Judith Vigna

ALBERT WHITMAN & COMPANY, NILES, ILLINOIS

For my mother

Library of Congress Cataloging-in-Publication Data

Vigna, Judith.
Boot weather/written and illustrated by Judith Vigna.
p. cm.
Summary: A little girl playing in her favorite boots in the snowy
backyard imagines herself in many adventurous situations.
ISBN 0-8075-0837-3 (lib. bdg.)
[1. Snow—Fiction. 2. Imagination—Fiction. 3. Play—Fiction.]
I. Title.   88-20563
PZ7.V67Bo 1989   CIP
[E]—dc19   AC

Text and illustrations © 1989 by Judith Vigna.
Published in 1989 by Albert Whitman & Company,
5747 W. Howard, Niles, Illinois 60648.
Published simultaneously in Canada by
General Publishing, Limited, Toronto.
All rights reserved. Printed in the United States of America.
10 9 8 7 6 5 4 3 2 1

When Kim's father comes in
and shouts "Boot weather!"
Kim can step into her favorite boots
and go anywhere she likes—

up hills

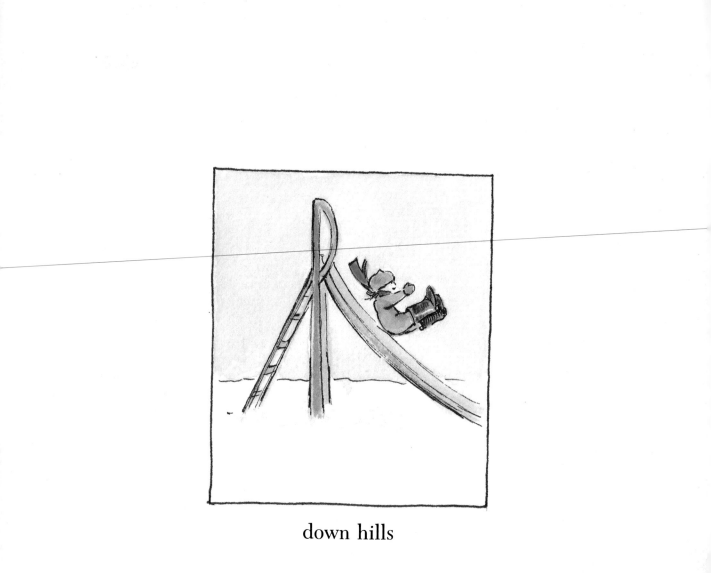

down hills

over rocks

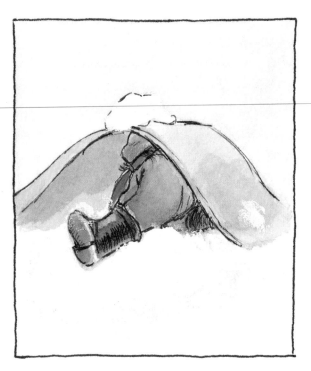

under bridges

in holes

out holes

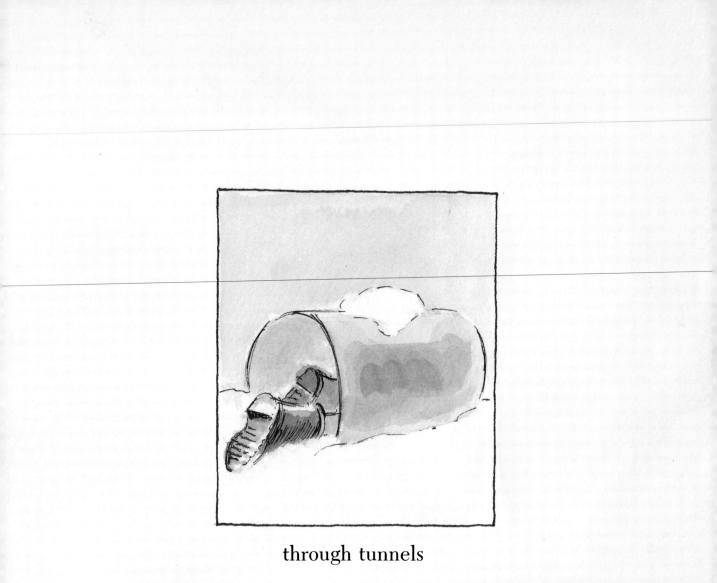

through tunnels

across ice

beside fences

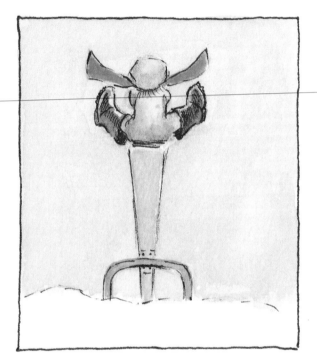

above snow

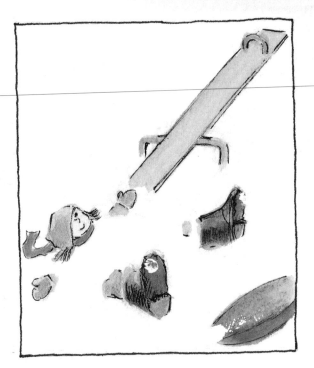

below snow.

In boot weather Kim can go
anywhere at all . . .

and still be home for lunch.